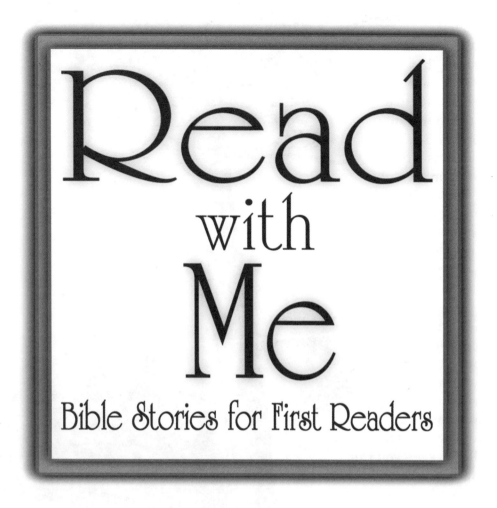

Read with Me

Bible Stories for First Readers

How To Use This Book

Enjoy sharing this storybook with your child. The book has two parts: one for your child and one for you. The children's story is written in larger print on the right-hand side. The adult text is written in smaller print on the left-hand side. The adult text will offer suggestions, explanations, and helps for ways you can use this storybook to share your faith with your young child.

Take time to read the adult text before reading the story to your child. This will help you familiarize yourself with the ideas and explanations that correspond with the story line. It will also keep you from being distracted by the adult text when you share the story with your child.

As children grow in body, they also grow in faith. You will have many opportunities to help your child deepen his or her relationship with God. We hope that sharing this storybook with your child is one of those opportunities.

Hold your child close beside you as you read. Let him or her feel the warmth of your touch and love as you experience together the wonder of God's creation.

In the Beginning

Written by Judy Newman-St. John
Illustrated by Charles Jakubowski

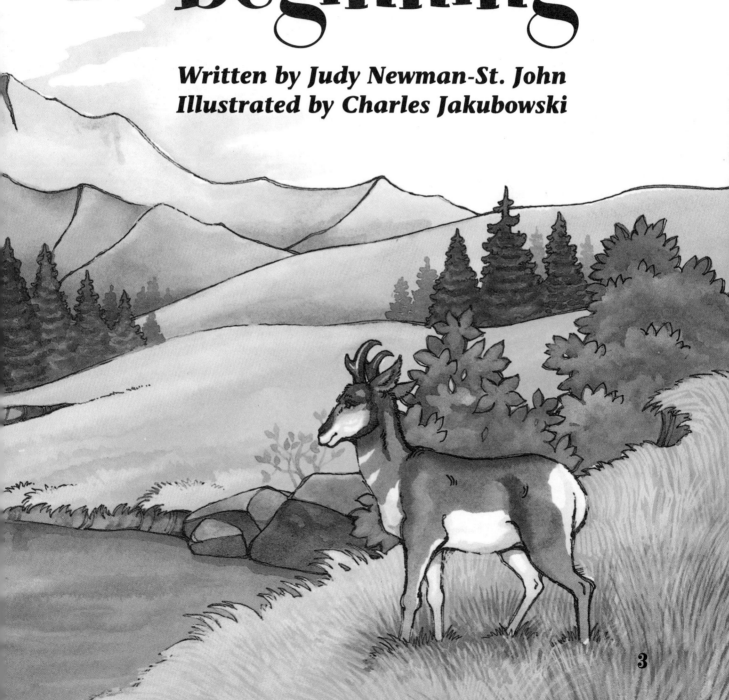

Young children learn about God's natural world by experiencing it directly. They learn not through books and logic, but through their senses. By using their eyes, ears, noses, tongues, and fingers they can discover that God's creation is real and important to them.

Hold the Bible as you begin to talk with your child about God's creation. Help your child to understand that the Bible tells us about creation.

Begin to experience God's world with your child; go outdoors and explore. Talk with your child about what you see. Invite him or her to tell you about each thing you see and to tell you why it is an important part of creation.

Take a blanket with you. Invite your child to lay on his or her back and look around. Talk about what you see. Lay on your stomach and make a frame with your hands. Place your hands on the grass and look through the frame. Talk about what you see.

Give thanks with your child for the wonderful world God has created.

4

In the beginning,
In the beginning,
God created the world,
  a world to see.
Sunshine and rainbows,
Mountains and meadows,
Honeysuckle and bees, zzzzz
Weeping willow trees.

Look, it's good.

5

Learning how to listen is an important step in learning for young children. Learning how to listen is not only essential for a child to learn how to follow directions, but it is also important for reading. Listening to how words sound when they are read aloud can help a child learn to associate different sounds with the letters and words printed on the page.

Listening is another way to learn about God's creation. Go outdoors with your child. Find a comfortable place to sit. Ask your child to close his or her eyes with you while you do the same. Be very quiet to permit concentration. Ask your child to name all the sounds he or she hears. Is there an animal nearby? Is a breeze rustling leaves in a tree? Is everything completely quiet?

Encourage your child to give thanks to God with you for all the sounds in God's creation.

In the beginning,
In the beginning,
God created the world, a world to hear.
Polar bears and arctic fox,
Snowy owls *Whoo, whoo* and musk ox.
Wolves and lemmings,
Whales that sing.

Listen, it's good.

Tasting food is a daily part of your young child's experiences. As with other sensory experiences, tasting food is one way to gain knowledge.

Talk with your child about foods she or he likes to taste. Ask your child to describe the taste and the feel of the food. Ask her or him to describe the way the food looks. By doing this he or she is combining different sensory experiences and is growing.

Experiment with different tastes. If your child is not afraid to try, let her or him wear a blindfold to taste different foods. The sense of taste will be heightened.

Let your child enjoy the names of foods and the tastes of foods (even the ones not many people like!).

Ask your child: Why do you imagine that God created this food?

Pray with your child, thanking God for all the foods in God's creation.

8

In the beginning,
In the beginning,
God created the world,
  a world to taste.
Oranges *Yummm* and lemons,
Limes and persimmons.
Coconuts and mangoes,
Green avocados.

Taste, it's good.

9

Young children are surrounded by a world of smells. Many smells trigger an emotion, a memory, or a need. Help your child to understand that there are many smells in God's creation.

Explore inside your home for objects that have a natural smell. Let your child tell you about different smells he or she finds.

Go outdoors. Enjoy searching for objects that have different smells.

If your child is willing, let him or her wear a blindfold to experience different smells. (Children can also use their hands to cover their eyes if they are uncomfortable with a blindfold.) The sense of smell will be heightened.

Ask: What is this smell? How does this smell make you feel? What does it remind you of?

Pray with your child, thanking God for all the different smells in God's creation.

In the beginning,
In the beginning,
God created the world,
  a world to smell.
Lilacs and raindrops,
Roses and forget-me-nots.
Skunks and stinkbugs *puuu*,
Grandma's hugs.

Smell, it's good.

Young children love tactile experiences. They love to reach into a bag and feel an object to guess what the object is. They love to feel items they can touch and manipulate.

Talk with your child about all the things she or he can feel. Help your child describe things as warm, cold, soft, rough, hard, squishy, flat, round, and so forth.

Go outdoors and explore the natural world around you. Let your child hold and manipulate items that are safe and describe them to you.

Give thanks with your child for the way God's wonderful world feels when touched.

In the beginning,
In the beginning,
God created the world,
 a world to feel.
Wet sand and cool water *splasssh*,
Seashells and sand dollars.
Warm sun and soft breeze,
Sunburned knees!

Feel, it's good.

13

As young children learn about God's creation, they learn about God's love and care. They learn about God's care through you and through others who provide for their needs. Your love will model God's love to them.

Your child is just beginning to learn about God's dependability. The cycle of the seasons can be a hard concept for your child to understand. Your child may view time in segments, rather than as an orderly progression of events. Time may be largely personal time, viewed here and now.

Your child does understand patterning. Help him or her understand the seasons and day and night as times when certain things happen. As your child understands the seasons and day and night, you can help him or her to understand the dependability of God's creation.

Take advantage of spontaneous moments to explore God's world with your child and thank God for all you see, hear, taste, smell, and touch.

14

In the beginning,
In the beginning,
God created the world,
   a world to know.
Morning and evening,
Winter and spring,
Summer and fall,
God loves us all.

Know, it's good.
Thank you, God.

15

In the beginning, God created.
Genesis 1:1

Who Dared? Joshua Dared!

18

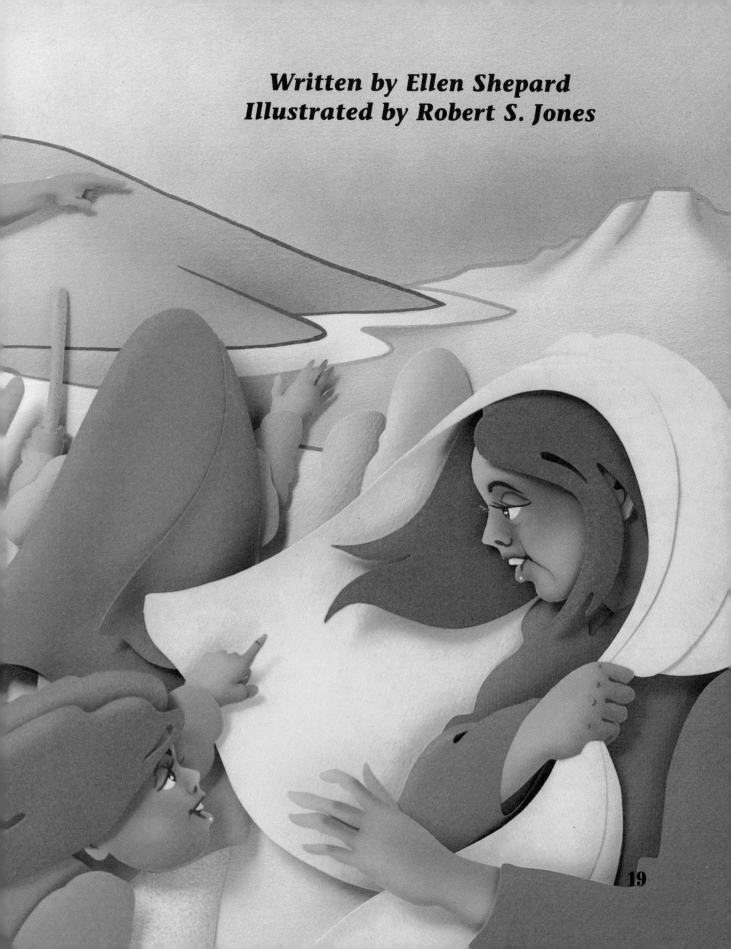

Written by Ellen Shepard
Illustrated by Robert S. Jones

19

Before you begin the story, talk with your child about Moses. Set the stage for the story. Explain that in this story Moses is very old. The Hebrew people have been wandering in the desert for a long time—forty years! God has promised the Hebrew people a special place to live, the Promised Land. Before they get to the Promised Land, the Hebrew people have to cross the Jordan River.

20

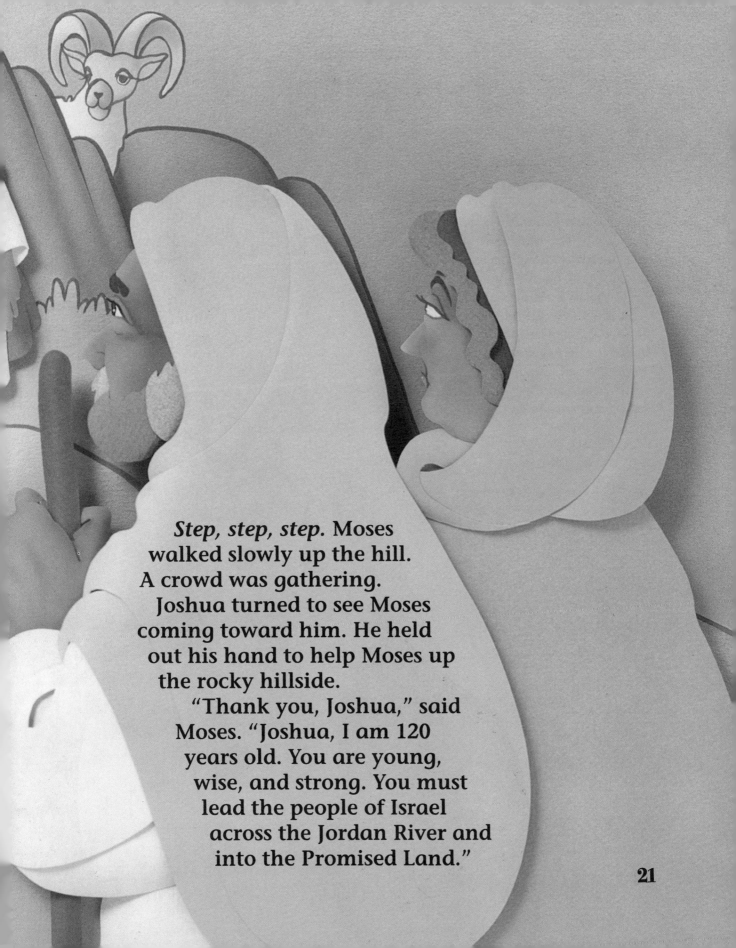

Step, step, step. Moses walked slowly up the hill. A crowd was gathering. Joshua turned to see Moses coming toward him. He held out his hand to help Moses up the rocky hillside.

"Thank you, Joshua," said Moses. "Joshua, I am 120 years old. You are young, wise, and strong. You must lead the people of Israel across the Jordan River and into the Promised Land."

Help your child to understand that to dare means to have the courage required for something you must do.

Explain that Joshua is a hero of the Old Testament. Joshua had an important job and a lot of responsibility. Joshua was afraid that he was not brave enough to do the job. Yet God told him to be "brave and courageous."

Talk with your child about what it means to be brave and courageous. Talk about the hard things that children and adults sometimes have to do that require bravery or courage.

Moses turned to the people. "God has chosen Joshua to be your new leader."

"Hooray! Hooray!" shouted the people.

Joshua looked at the cheering crowd. Joshua looked at Moses. He knew that leaders were supposed to be strong and brave.

Do I dare to be their leader? wondered Joshua.

Help your child to understand that he or she will continue to learn throughout his or her lifetime. Help your child to understand that even adults still learn from others.

Explain that Moses had helped Joshua to learn many things that would help him be a good leader. Most important of all, Moses had helped Joshua to trust God.

Talk with your child about ways we can trust God. Share stories about important people who have helped you and/or your child learn to trust God.

24

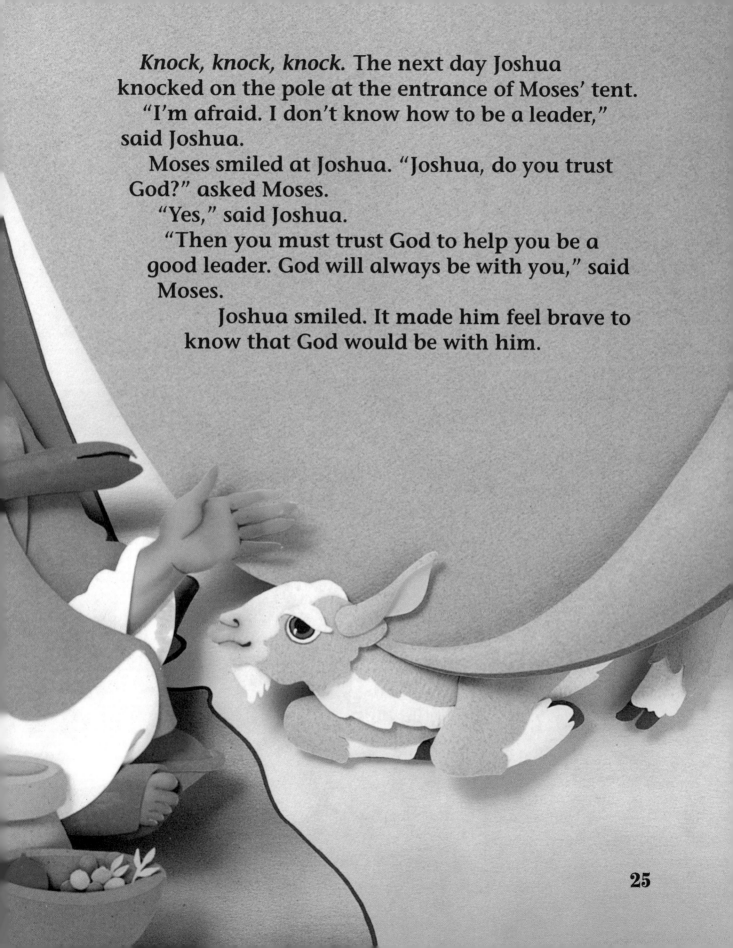

Knock, knock, knock. The next day Joshua knocked on the pole at the entrance of Moses' tent.

"I'm afraid. I don't know how to be a leader," said Joshua.

Moses smiled at Joshua. "Joshua, do you trust God?" asked Moses.

"Yes," said Joshua.

"Then you must trust God to help you be a good leader. God will always be with you," said Moses.

Joshua smiled. It made him feel brave to know that God would be with him.

Help your child to imagine what life would have been like in Old Testament times. Talk about tents and animals and ways of travel (mostly walking). Point out details in the illustration on these pages.

Explain that the ark of the covenant was a special box that contained God's laws. The people were wandering in the desert and had no church building where they could worship. The ark of the covenant was important to them like our church is important to us today.

26

Splash, splash, splash.
Joshua walked along the edge of the Jordan River.

"Joshua, it is time for you to lead the Hebrew people across the Jordan River and into the land I promised you," said God.

Joshua nodded his head. He went to the people and told them to fold up their tents. He asked the priests to carry the ark of the covenant, the special box that held the Ten Commandments.

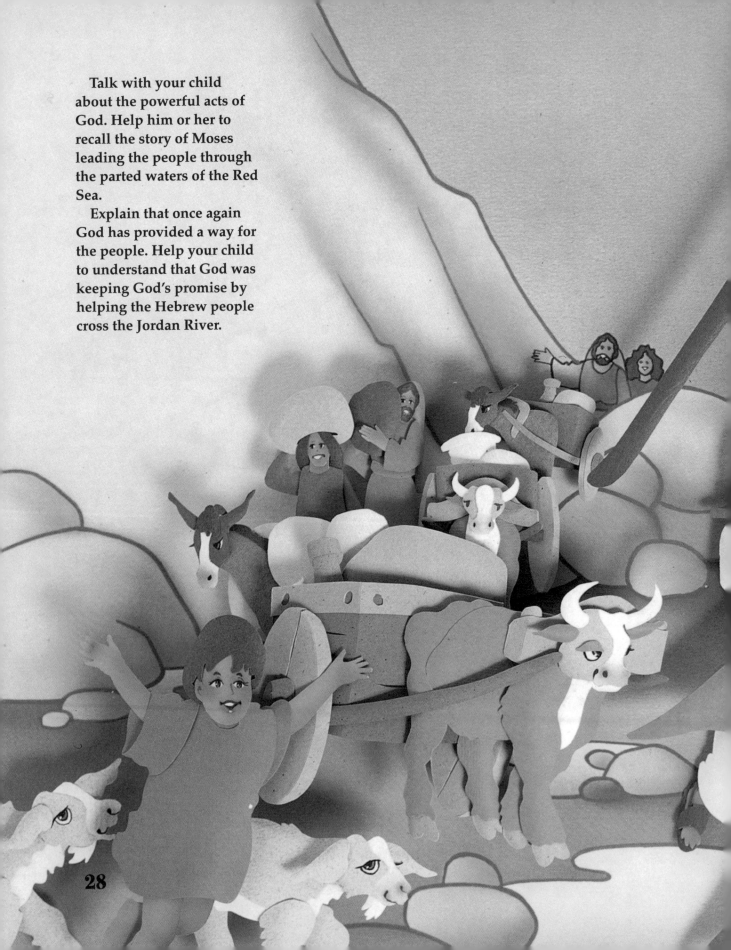

Talk with your child about the powerful acts of God. Help him or her to recall the story of Moses leading the people through the parted waters of the Red Sea.

Explain that once again God has provided a way for the people. Help your child to understand that God was keeping God's promise by helping the Hebrew people cross the Jordan River.

28

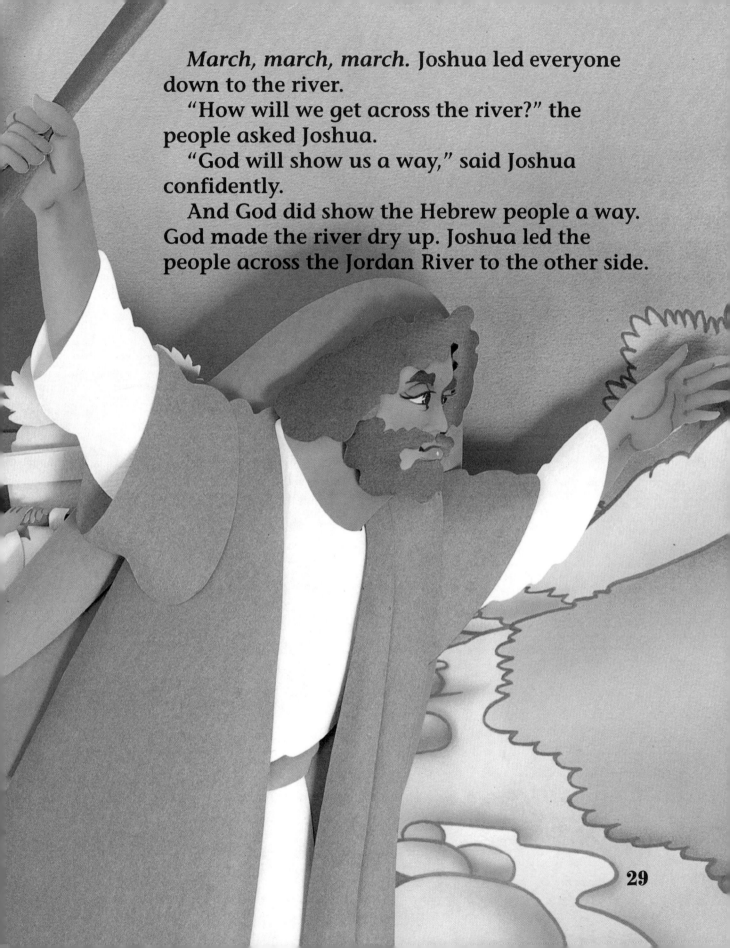

March, march, march. Joshua led everyone down to the river.

"How will we get across the river?" the people asked Joshua.

"God will show us a way," said Joshua confidently.

And God did show the Hebrew people a way. God made the river dry up. Joshua led the people across the Jordan River to the other side.

Help your child imagine how it might feel to be away from home for a long, long time. Help him or her to understand that God was giving the people a new home in the land that God had promised them.

Talk with your child about the wonderful things God has provided for you and your child. Say a prayer of thanks to God with your child.

Assure your child that God is always with us and helps us to have the courage to do all the things God wants us to do.

30

"We must remember what God has done for us," Joshua told the people. "A leader from each tribe will take a stone from the Jordan River and place the stone at the edge of the Promised Land."

Thwack, thwack, thwack. As the priests piled the stones, Joshua gave thanks to God.

"Thank you, God, for being with us," Joshua prayed. "And thank you for giving me the courage to dare to lead your people."

Who dared to be a leader for God? Joshua dared!

31

A Song of David

Written by Sheila Allison
Illustrated by Kersti Frigell

34

Sheep were probably the most important domestic animal during David's time. They provided wool, skins, meat, milk, fat, and horns. Bible-times people also used sheep for sacrifices. It was David's responsibility to take care of his family's sheep.

This was no easy task; the life of the shepherd could be very lonely. David spent much of his life away from home, exposed to the weather and the dangers of the wild.

Even though David was very young, he took his responsibilities quite seriously. Talk with your child about his or her responsibilities and express how much you appreciate what your child does; for example, picking up toys or helping to feed a pet. Give your child an opportunity to express his or her feelings about those responsibilities.

David was the youngest in his family. He didn't get to spend much time with his brothers. But David's father, Jesse, had given David an important job. Jesse asked David to tend the family's sheep.

David's tasks included leading the sheep to food and water and keeping the flock safe. The sheep had a tendency to wander off; and without a shepherd to protect them, the sheep were easy prey. At night he counted each sheep as it entered the sheepfold and then went in search of any that were missing.

After the sheep were settled, David sat on the hillside, playing his harp and singing his praises to God. Talk with your child about quiet times for praising God. Talk about places where we can praise God. Share with your child some of your quiet-times experiences for praising God.

David was a good shepherd. He protected the sheep from lions and bears. Even though he watched the flock in the fields, David still had time to play his harp, to write songs, and to talk to God. God knew what David was like on the inside; God knew what was in David's heart.

David was inspired by his surroundings as he acknowledged God's creation. Talk with your child about the beauty of creation around you. Ask: What do you hear? see? taste? feel?

Pray with your child, thanking God for our senses and for all the beauty surrounding us.

While he was in the field one day, David heard the water bubbling in a nearby stream. *Blub, blub, blub.* He heard the birds chirping. *Tweet, tweet, tweet!* There were also bees buzzing. *Buzz, buzz, buzz!* David felt the breeze blowing. *Whew, whew, whew.* And of course, he heard the sheep. *Baa, baa, baa!*

One of the praises David
sang, Psalm 23, is still a
favorite today. In Psalm 23
David compares God to a
loving shepherd who watches
over his sheep and takes care
of all their needs. David
viewed his relationship with
God in the same way and had
the steadfast trust in God that
a sheep has in its shepherd.

Talk with your child about
your feelings of trust in God.
Name the ways you trust God.

42

David played his harp while he listened to all the sounds around him. He began to make up words to go with the tune he was strumming. The young shepherd sang to his flock, "The Lord is my shepherd." *Strum, strum, strum.*

43

Explain that David played the harp and sang songs as a way of praising God. Give your child the opportunity to experience a variety of ways of praising God. Let him or her be noisy, then quiet. Let him or her sing, dance, shout, sit quietly, play musical instruments, wave scarfs, paint, color, and pray to express praise to God.

David kept on singing and strumming. The sheep looked up at the young boy. The sheep looked at each other. "I have everything I need," sang David. *Strum, strum, strum.*

45

David knew God's love and trusted in God's care for him. David's time alone in the hills must have given him time to develop an inner strength and a relationship with God. This inner strength that God discerned in David and in David's love for God set him apart to be the chosen king.

Help your child understand that God knows us and is with us at all times and in all places. Assure your child of God's tender love and care.

46

Then David played a different tune. The sheep were still listening. David strummed and hummed, strummed and hummed. Then he thought of words to go with the new tune. "Trust in the Lord and do good," sang David, the shepherd boy.

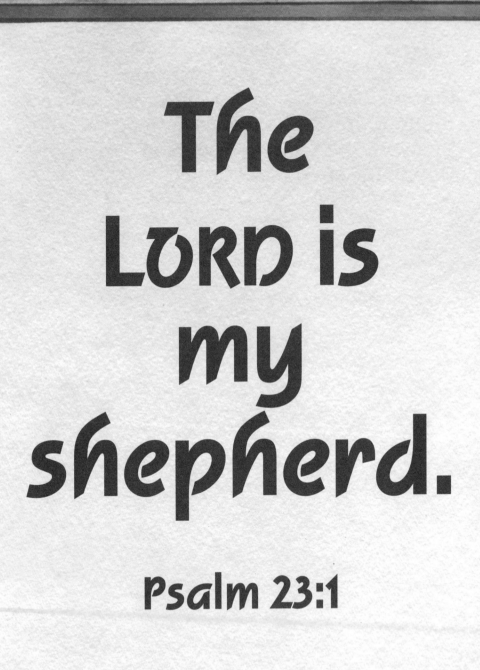

The Lord is my shepherd.

Psalm 23:1

Ruth: A Story of God's Love

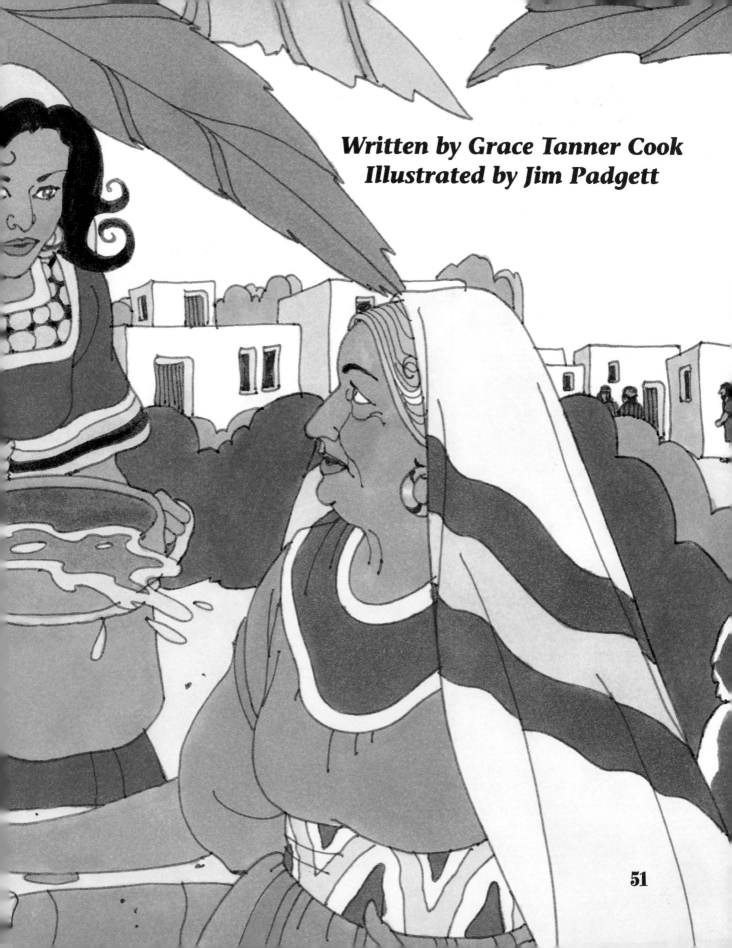

Written by Grace Tanner Cook
Illustrated by Jim Padgett

51

Before reading this story with your child, help him or her understand who Naomi and Ruth were and how they were related. Extended family relationships are sometimes difficult for young children to understand. Use examples from your own family, if possible, to help your child comprehend the relationship between a mother and a daughter-in-law.

Naomi, who was the mother-in-law in the story, had moved from Judah to Moab with her husband, Elimelech, and two sons to find food. While living in Moab, her sons married Ruth and Orpah.

After a few years, Naomi's husband and sons died. Naomi was upset and angry with God. She had no grandchildren and wanted to return to Bethlehem to live out her old age.

Naomi loved her daughters-in-law, Orpah and Ruth, and wanted them to be happy. Out of love, Naomi encouraged Orpah and Ruth to return to their families. Orpah chose to return to her family, but Ruth chose to stay with Naomi.

Splash, splash, splash. The water in the bucket splashed as Ruth pulled it from the well. She and her mother-in-law, Naomi, wanted a drink of water.

Naomi smiled at Ruth. "I must return to my relatives in Bethlehem," Naomi said. "You must go back to your family in Moab."

True family love is unconditional. Ruth dearly loved Naomi and could not imagine life without her. From the depths of her heart Ruth begged to go with Naomi to Bethlehem. She was willing to adopt a foreign country, ". . . your people shall be my people"; embrace the worship of one God, ". . . your God, my God"; and remain with Naomi until death, ". . . where you die, I will die." There can hardly be a stronger expression of love.

Young children live in many different family structures. Whether your child's family experience is that of a nuclear family, a blended family, or an extended family, children should realize that family love and care are very special. Family is one way God expresses God's love for us. Talk with your child about ways love is expressed in your family.

54

Sob, sob, sob. Tears ran down Ruth's cheeks as she hugged Naomi.

"I love you, Naomi," Ruth cried. "I want to go with you to Bethlehem. I will take care of you there, and I will worship your God."

The two women were poor and had no way to support themselves. The law code of Deuteronomy 24:19-21 allowed a needy stranger or widow to gather in the fields what grain was left by the harvesters. Feeling responsible for their livelihood, Ruth volunteered to go to the fields and gather grain.

Help your child understand that life in Bible times was very different from life today. Explain that when Ruth and Naomi moved, they traveled on foot and carried few belongings. They moved into a small, one-room, mud-brick house with no furniture. They slept on a rug or straw mat. They prepared their own foods. Help your child make comparisons between life today and life in Bible times.

Step, step, step. Ruth and Naomi walked to Bethlehem together. When they got there, they had no money to buy food.

Naomi and Ruth were hungry. "Don't worry," Ruth told Naomi. "I will gather grain from the fields. We will make bread."

Since Ruth gathered leftover grain it took all day to collect enough for bread. Bending and stooping under the hot sun was tiring work, and as a foreigner, there was a great risk of someone harming her. To Ruth, gathering grain was a labor of love and a means of support for Naomi and herself. News of Ruth's kindness to Naomi spread through Bethlehem. The field workers shared this information with Boaz.

Gathering grain and making bread was vital to biblical life. Women spent many hours making bread. Share with your child how grain becomes bread. Women ground grain between two stones. The upper stone was rounded, and it ground the grain on the lower saddle-shaped stone into a coarse flour. Women mixed the flour with water, and yeast (or leaven) was used to raise it. After the dough rose, it was shaped into small, flat cakes and placed on a round piece of clay. The bread was baked in outdoor clay ovens.

58

Scoop, scoop, scoop. Ruth used her hands to scoop grain from the ground to fill her bag. Ruth worked hard all day long.

Boaz saw how hard Ruth worked to gather grain for herself and her mother-in-law, Naomi.

59

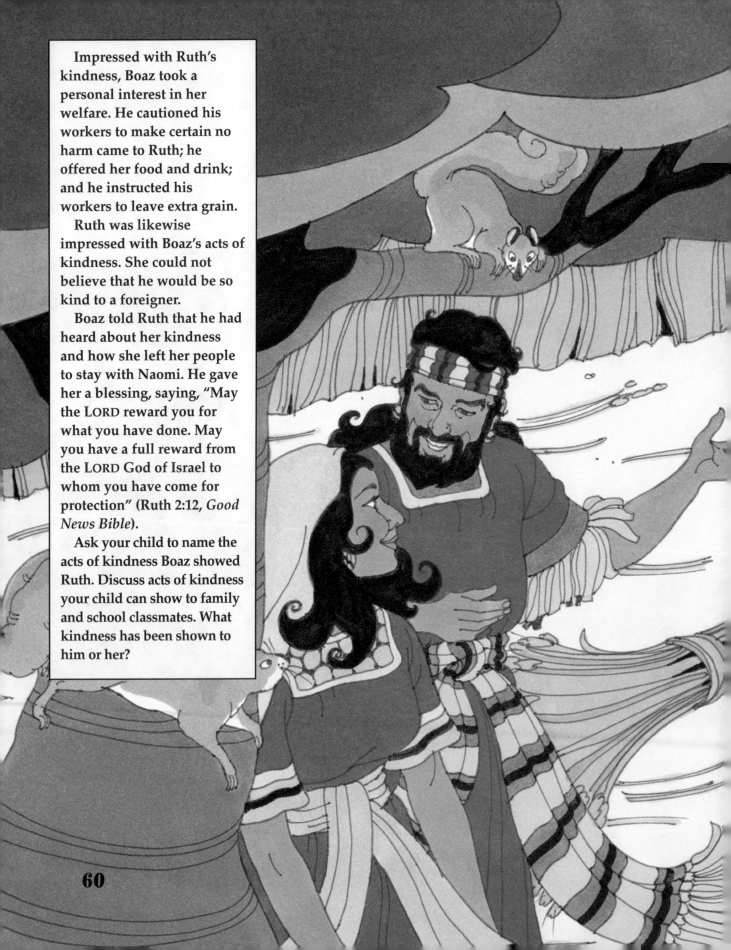

Impressed with Ruth's kindness, Boaz took a personal interest in her welfare. He cautioned his workers to make certain no harm came to Ruth; he offered her food and drink; and he instructed his workers to leave extra grain.

Ruth was likewise impressed with Boaz's acts of kindness. She could not believe that he would be so kind to a foreigner.

Boaz told Ruth that he had heard about her kindness and how she left her people to stay with Naomi. He gave her a blessing, saying, "May the LORD reward you for what you have done. May you have a full reward from the LORD God of Israel to whom you have come for protection" (Ruth 2:12, *Good News Bible*).

Ask your child to name the acts of kindness Boaz showed Ruth. Discuss acts of kindness your child can show to family and school classmates. What kindness has been shown to him or her?

Work, work, work. Ruth worked hard gathering grain.

"Ruth," said Boaz, "you may gather grain from my fields, drink water from my water jars, and eat bread with my workers."

Ruth smiled in surprise. "Thank you for your kindness," she said.

After hearing the news of Boaz's kindness, Naomi became overjoyed and thankful. She was still looking for a sign that God had not forsaken her. She also wanted a husband for Ruth.

According to marriage law (Deuteronomy 25:5-6), the brother or nearest kin of a deceased man must marry the widow. The first-born son would rank as the son of the deceased man. As time went on, Boaz, a relative of Naomi, exercised his kinship rights, purchased Naomi's property, and took Ruth to be his wife.

A son named Obed was born to Ruth and Boaz. There was much rejoicing in Bethlehem over the birth! Through the unselfish love of Ruth and Boaz, Naomi received God's blessing.

Talk with your child about babies and how much joy is felt when babies are born.

As time went on, Boaz grew to love Ruth, and he married her. *Waa, waa, waa.* Ruth gave birth to a baby boy named Obed. All of Bethlehem celebrated! Ruth, Boaz, and Naomi knew that God had blessed their family.

63

Be kind to one another.

Ephesians 4:32

64

Elijah: A Man Who Listened to God

Written by MaryJane Pierce Norton
Illustrated by Benton Mahan

Elijah was a prophet who had a strong faith in God. At the time when he lived, there was a struggle going on between people who believed and worshiped the one true God and people who believed and worshiped Baal, a god of the Canaanites.

Elijah has remained for centuries a strong reminder of those who stand firm in their faith. Elijah serves as an example of a man who worshiped God, who listened to God, and who carried out God's instructions even when it meant discomfort or harm to himself. In fact, the name *Elijah* means "Jehovah is my God."

Talk with your child about the persons in your community or your church who have a very strong faith in God. What are these persons like? Help your child name qualities or actions of a person who has a strong faith.

68

Elijah was a man who loved God. Because he loved God, he listened to God. Elijah talked with God in prayer and followed the laws that God had given to the people. Elijah often felt very alone.

"Does anyone else still worship God?" he wondered.

King Ahab had married
Queen Jezebel, a Phoenician
(or Canaanite) princess. She
brought with her a devotion
to the gods of her country,
the chief of which was Baal.
Now Ahab could have
remained strong in his faith
to God, but he didn't. He
allowed Jezebel to enforce
worship of Baal with the
Israelite people. The irony in
this story is that Baal was the
storm god. So God's
bringing the drought really
showed the powerlessness of
the Phoenician gods.

After delivering the
message of the drought to
Ahab, Elijah had to leave the
land and stay in a place
outside of Ahab's
jurisdiction.

Talk with your child about
how difficult it is to stand up
to someone who is powerful.
Think together about the
traits Elijah had that made
him able to go to King Ahab.
You might list traits such as
courage, fearlessness, a
feeling of being right, and
knowing God was with him.

Two people who did not worship God were King Ahab and
Queen Jezebel.

God sent Elijah to tell King Ahab, "God says there will be
no rain in Israel."

This made King Ahab very angry. He was so angry that
Elijah had to leave the country and find a safe place to hide.

There were many miraculous things that happened to Elijah. These were signs of how much God watched over him.

The story of Elijah's stay at Cherith Brook is one of those miracles (1 Kings 17:1-7). By hiding near the brook, Elijah was assured of water to drink. Food was another matter. The Bible says that God sent ravens in the morning with bread and meat for Elijah to eat. The ravens returned at night with more of the same foods.

Children may ask how the ravens were able to bring bread and meat to Elijah. There is no explanation of how this happened. The Bible simply tells us it happened. You might want to ask your child to think about what it might have been like to be Elijah. Talk about how Elijah might have felt as he waited for the ravens, as he watched the clouds, as he drank from the brook.

72

Elijah came to a brook, and God
told him to stay there. He had water
to drink from the brook.

Every day some black birds,
which are called ravens, brought
Elijah bread and meat. This way
Elijah had food and water. But
soon there was no more water
in the brook because there
was no rain.

Next we have another of God's miracles. Again, we learn that God was taking care of Elijah.

After the brook dried up, God sent Elijah to the town of Zarephath to find a widow who would feed him (1 Kings 17:8-16). This was a town in Phoenicia, so the woman was not even an Israelite, but she listened to God. This helps us remember that the Israelites were not the only recipients of God's care.

Although the woman must have thought Elijah was crazy to ask for food when she obviously needed the little she had, she did what he asked. And God miraculously replenished her ingredients to make bread with during the length of the drought.

Help your child think of the ways he or she can show kindness to others. Think together about people who need our care.

God then sent Elijah to a town. When Elijah reached the town, he saw a woman gathering some sticks to make a fire.

"Please bring me some water and something to eat," Elijah said to the woman.

Even though she didn't have very much food, the woman did as Elijah asked.

God made sure that Elijah, the woman, and her son had enough to eat.

Part of the Elijah story is not covered in the story for children. There was a confrontation between Elijah and the prophets of Baal. The prophets of Baal energetically called forth their god to start a fire at an altar. But nothing happened. Elijah then called upon God and the sacrifice was consumed. In seeing this, many people confessed that the Lord was God. The prophets of Baal were defeated and killed. The final scene is the coming of the long-awaited rain. This infuriated Jezebel. So once again Elijah had to flee (1 Kings 18:25–1 Kings 19:3).

Think again of Elijah's feelings. He's leaving the country again. He is fearful for his life. He feels alone. And he would like to quit. But he keeps on, with God's help.

Talk together about times when you have been fearful, alone, and sad. How does knowing that God is with you help during those times? Ask your child to think about times when praying to God helps her or him.

King Ahab and Queen Jezebel were still angry at Elijah. They were angry because God had caused the drought, the time when there was no rain. Even after the rain started again, the king and queen were still angry.

Elijah had to run away again. He felt very sorry for himself. "Please, God," Elijah prayed, "this is too hard. I don't know what to do anymore."

Elijah climbed Mount Sinai and found a cave to hide in. There, he was waiting for God. Elijah prayed desperately: "Take away my life; I might as well be dead . . . I am the only one left—and they are trying to kill me" (1 Kings 19:4, 10, *Good News Bible*).

While Elijah was on the mountain, he witnessed some incredible acts: a mighty wind; an earthquake; a big fire. Elijah could have expected God to be in any of these. But when Elijah finally hears God speaking to him, it is in a whisper, a still, small voice.

Sometimes we look for God in big and spectacular ways. Sometimes we forget to look for God in small things. Talk with your child about the small things that remind you of God.

God goes on to tell Elijah what to do and reminds Elijah that others have been faithful to God too. God reminds Elijah that he is not alone.

Elijah walked to Mount Sinai and went into a cave. Elijah heard a strong wind. Then he felt the earth shake and rumble. Then he saw a big fire. After the fire, everything was very, very quiet. While it was still quiet, Elijah heard a voice whispering.

Elijah went out and stood at the entrance of the cave. God told him what to do next. Elijah obeyed God. Elijah was thankful that God had not forgotten him. Elijah knew that God would always help him.

GOD CARES FOR YOU

1 Peter 5:7, adapted

80

A Baby Is Coming

Written by Daphna Flegal
Illustrated by Cheryl Arnemann

83

Talk with your child about preparing for a long trip. Encourage your child to tell you what he or she would need or want to take.

Have you ever taken a trip with your child? Remind your child about the trip. If you have not traveled with your child, plan a pretend trip. Let your child imagine where you will go and how you will travel.

84

"Do you think we have everything we need?" Mary asked Joseph as she packed some fruit and bread in a bag.

"Yes, I think so," Joseph said as he smiled at Mary. "We have food, water, clothes, and blankets. I'm glad you reminded me to get feed for the donkey so he won't be hungry on our long journey to Bethlehem."

85

Have your child find the donkey in the picture. Ask your child to show you how a donkey walks or how a donkey sounds. Ask your child how it might feel to ride a donkey for a long time.

Compare Mary and Joseph's journey with the donkey to how we travel in cars and airplanes today. Ask your child how it feels to ride in a car for a long time.

86

Clippity clop, clippity clop. Carefully the donkey stepped around the rocks as he walked down the dusty road.

"How do you feel, Mary? Are you tired?" Joseph asked as he walked beside Mary.

"A little," Mary said. "I've been thinking about our baby. I know he will be a special baby and we will love him very much."

"Yes," said Joseph. "The angel told us to name him Jesus."

Help your child understand that an inn is similar to the motels and hotels we have today. Ask your child to imagine how Mary and Joseph felt when the innkeeper told them there was no room to stay in the inn. Then ask your child to imagine how Mary and Joseph felt when the innkeeper said they could stay in the stable.

88

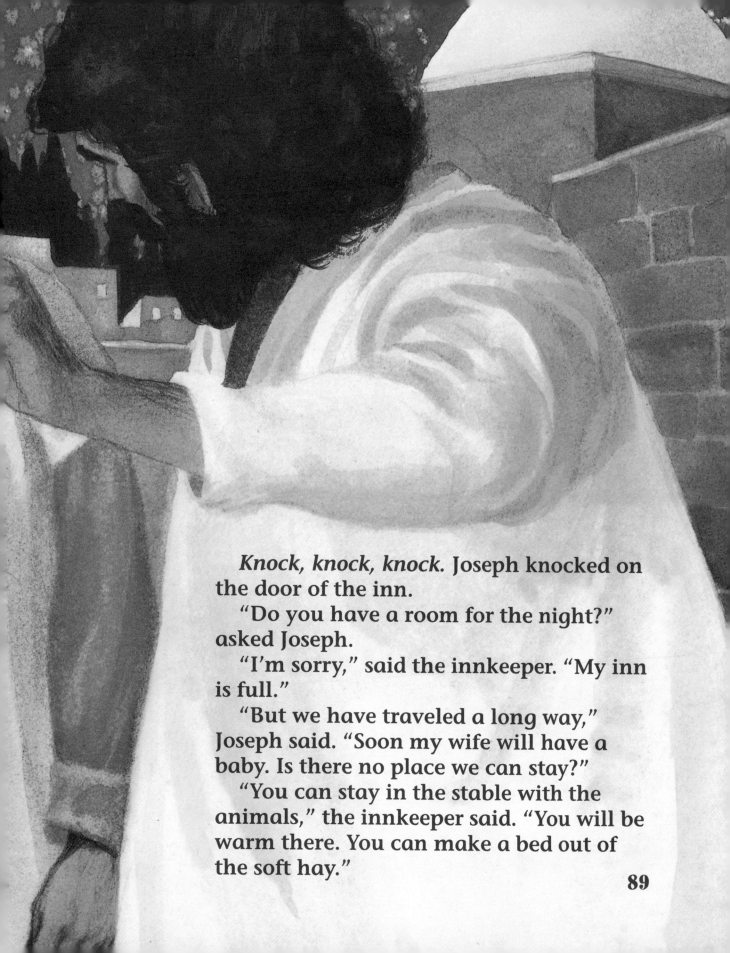

Knock, knock, knock. Joseph knocked on the door of the inn.

"Do you have a room for the night?" asked Joseph.

"I'm sorry," said the innkeeper. "My inn is full."

"But we have traveled a long way," Joseph said. "Soon my wife will have a baby. Is there no place we can stay?"

"You can stay in the stable with the animals," the innkeeper said. "You will be warm there. You can make a bed out of the soft hay."

89

Describe the stable as a place like a barn where animals are kept. Encourage your child to make the sounds of the animals at the stable.

90

Mary and Joseph were happy to have a warm place to sleep. Joseph made a bed out of the soft hay.

"Are you warm enough?" Joseph asked as he covered Mary with a blanket.

"Thank you, Joseph," answered Mary. "Now I am nice and warm." Mary laid down on the bed of hay.

M-o-o M-o-o. B-a-a B-a-a. Mary and Joseph went to sleep to the quiet sounds of the cow and sheep. Soon even the animals were asleep.

Talk with your child about her or his birth. Look at any pictures you have of your child as a newborn baby. Talk about what you did to care for your child when he or she was born.

92

Then something wonderful happened. Mary gave birth to her firstborn son. Mary wrapped the baby in soft bands of cloth to make him feel safe and warm.

Tell your child that God planned for Jesus to be born so that we might know God's love. One way we can see God's love is through the love of our family. Let your child know that you were happy when he or she was born. Say "I love you" to your child. Then say a prayer thanking God for your son or daughter and for baby Jesus.

94

"Oh, Joseph," said Mary, "he is such a
beautiful baby boy." Mary gently rocked her
son to sleep.

"Yes," said Joseph as he lovingly made a soft
bed of hay for the baby. Joseph took the
sleeping baby from Mary, kissed him, and
gently laid him in the manger.

Outside a bright star sparkled in the sky. Inside a small lamp cast a warm glow around the stable.

Mary and Joseph looked with wonder at the tiny baby sleeping in the hay. They remembered what the angel told them,

You are to name him Jesus.

Matthew 1:21

Tell Me the
Stories of Jesus

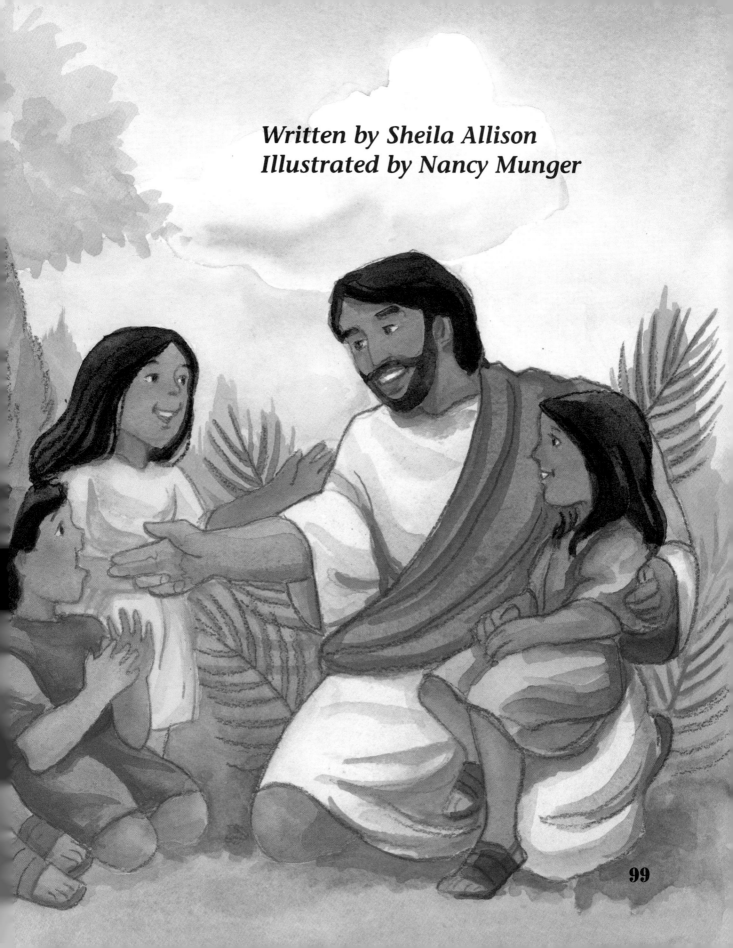

Written by Sheila Allison
Illustrated by Nancy Munger

The Christmas story is very familiar to us as parents and teachers. We can easily identify with the anticipation, hope, apprehension, and joy that Mary and Joseph felt so many years ago. These same emotions are experienced by young children, but they do not have the skills to identify and express these feelings.

Ask your child to tell you the Christmas story in her or his own words. Listen for pauses that might signal you to help with the transition. Praise your child for all that he or she remembers. Talk about the importance of remembering the *real* reason for the season. Explain that if Jesus had not been born, we would not celebrate Christmas.

Tell about your child's birth—time of day, weather, what city, who was at the hospital, and so forth. Show your child his or her newborn pictures.

100

Remember the special baby whose birth we celebrate on Christmas? That's right! Baby Jesus! Remember Mary, Joseph, the shepherds, the angels, the star in the sky, and the wise men? It's a happy story, isn't it? But there's MORE to the story of Jesus. MUCH MORE!

It is hard for children (as well as adults) to believe that they could have anything in common with Jesus. That's the beauty of God sending Jesus to be with us. Ask your child: "What games do you like to play? What games do you think Jesus played? What do you like to eat? What foods do you think Jesus liked?"

Children in Bible times liked to imitate what grownups did; they played weddings and funerals, and pretended to be chief elders who settled disputes among the people. Playing running games, leap frog, and marbles were favorite childhood activities. Some of the foods that children in Bible times probably ate included bread, cheese, grapes, raisins, dates, figs, almonds, olives, melons, honey, beans, peas, cucumbers, onions, fish (pickled fish was a favorite), lamb, and chicken.

Families did not eat breakfast, but children and old people took a piece of bread in the early morning before they went to the fields to work. At noon they ate a light meal. At the main meal in the evening the family sat on mats on the floor around a larger straw mat, which lay on the floor or was spread over a low wooden trestle. The food was placed in a large bowl in the center of the mat. Hands were washed before and after eating; the family members used their fingers instead of knives, forks, or spoons. The father said a blessing at the beginning and at the end of the meal.

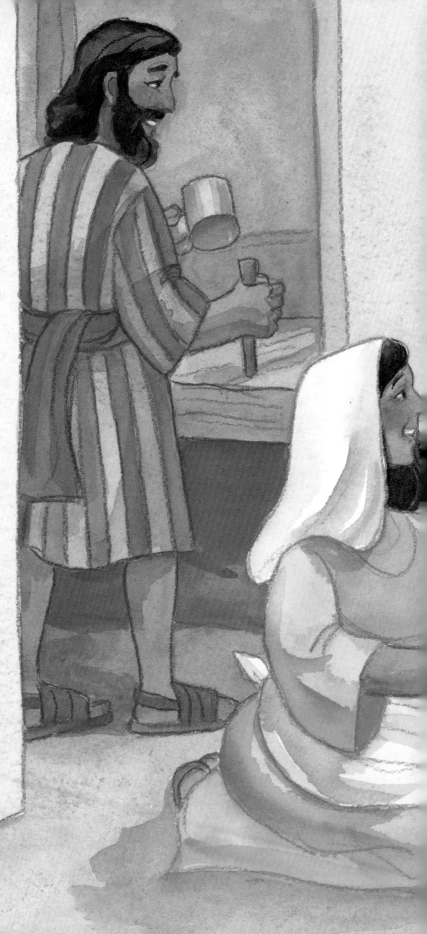

Jesus grew and grew. He learned
and played. He ate and slept. Jesus
did most everything children do as
they grow and learn—just like you!

In interpreting the story of Jesus talking with the teachers (priests) in the Temple, we often emphasize the fact that Mary and Joseph had already left Jerusalem and were on their way home when they realized that Jesus wasn't with them. As you tell this story, emphasize instead that Jesus was learning and that learning is an important part of growing up.

In Bible times, children were taught at home, first by their mother, then by their father. Many boys were then educated at synagogue schools starting at age six.

Ask your child to think about all the things that he or she has learned already—ABC's, counting, colors, name, address, nursery rhymes.

Sometimes Jesus went on trips with his family. Once when they were in Jerusalem, Jesus went to the Temple and talked with the teachers there. The teachers thought Jesus was a very smart boy.

Baptism marks a significant time in a person's life. Being baptized signals a new life as part of God's family. Talk with your child about baptism in your church today. Has your child witnessed a baptism? Do you have photos of a baptism that you can share with your child?

Jesus kept growing. When he became a
man, Jesus went to see John the Baptist. Jesus
asked John to baptize him, and John did.

The original twelve disciples were ordinary men who had occupations, families, personal strengths, and human weaknesses. But Jesus *chose* each one of them because he knew what kind of person each could become. Jesus could see a person's potential and love that person just as he or she was. The disciples were not sure what was ahead of them when they decided to follow Jesus, but they followed and they trusted him.

Ask your child to name some persons from your church—Sunday school classmates, older children, youth, adults, and older adults. Talk about the people who work at the church— pastors, secretary, custodian. Their work is very important, but they cannot do everything at the church. They need helpers. Think of people who help do the church's work and it's not their job; for example, teachers, choir members, directors, ushers. It takes many different people to do the work at church. Talk about ways that your child can help (bring offering, hand out bulletins, sing in choir, donate food or clothing).

Pray with your child: "Thank you, God, for all of the helpers who work at church. Thank you for letting me be a helper too. Amen."

Jesus knew that he had important work to do, but he could not do his work by himself. He needed helpers. Jesus chose twelve helpers, and he called them *disciples*.

Young children do not know the word *miracles*; they may know that Jesus healed sick people or gave sight to blind people. Talk with your child about times when she or he has been sick. What made your child feel better? (visitors, cards, a teddy bear, soup, Popsicles). What are some things your child can do to help someone who is sick feel better?

Sometimes Jesus would make a sick person well. The people were happy that Jesus was with them.

Jesus taught about God and God's love for everyone. Jesus said, "Love one another."

Love
one
another.

John 15:17

Come! Follow Me!

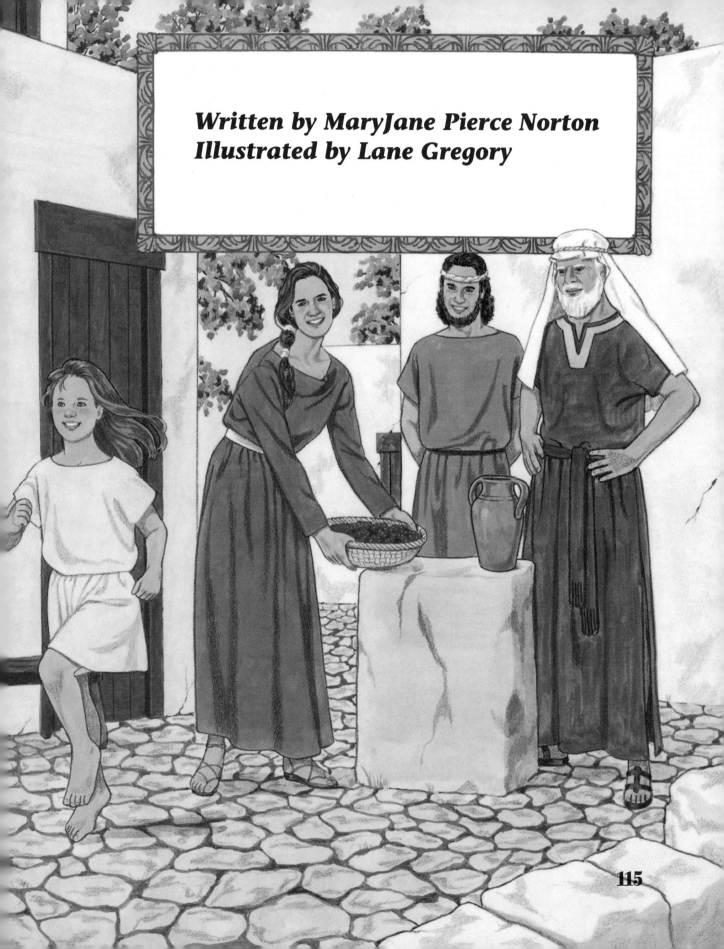

Written by MaryJane Pierce Norton
Illustrated by Lane Gregory

In the Gospel of Mark, the story of Jesus unfolds in an abrupt, fast-paced manner. Jesus is baptized. Jesus is tempted. Jesus begins his ministry. Jesus calls his followers. We don't have much information about what happened, what Jesus was thinking, or what Jesus was feeling. We can only imagine what we might have felt if we had lived when Jesus lived.

When Jesus was baptized, he recognized his very special relationship with God. Jesus must have known that from that time on his life would be very different. But Jesus did not begin his ministry immediately. First, he went to the wilderness where Jesus was alone with God—being tested, thinking, praying, and planning. He returned ready to teach and preach and call others to be his followers.

Although being quiet for any length of time may be difficult for your child, try adding some listening time to your times when you pray together.

116

Thwack, thwack, thwack. Jesus' sandals made a soft thwack sound as he walked quickly toward Galilee.

Jesus waved to his mother.

"Why are you in such a hurry?" asked Mary.

"God has many things for me to do," said Jesus. "I need helpers who can travel with me and help me tell people about God's love. I'm going to Galilee to find people who will come and follow me."

In the gospel accounts of the calling of the disciples, we have a picture of Jesus' power. When Jesus called Peter and Andrew, they simply put down their nets and followed. James and John left their boat and their father to follow Jesus. There is no record of any questioning on their part. Jesus called and they followed.

This message is not just for people in Bible times; it is also for people today. The gospel gives us examples of how to answer Jesus' call. Jesus calls. We follow. We, too, are asked to stop whatever we are doing and follow Jesus.

Talk with your child about how you and your family try to follow Jesus today. Help your child identify some of the things he or she can do to follow Jesus such as sharing when playing with others, praying to God at mealtime and at night, helping with tasks at home, and visiting people who may be lonely.

118

Splash, splash, splash. The waves of the Sea of Galilee splish-splashed as Jesus walked along the shore.

Jesus saw some fishermen working on their nets beside the Sea of Galilee.

"Peter, Andrew," called Jesus. "Come help me tell people about God."

The two men dropped their fishing nets and followed Jesus. Jesus saw two more fishermen, James and John.

"Follow me," said Jesus. And James and John followed Jesus too.

When Jesus called Levi to follow him, many people were shocked and puzzled. Generally tax collectors were not liked or trusted because they often cheated those from whom they collected. Many of Jesus' friends couldn't understand why Jesus was calling someone like Levi to be a part of his group.

As a tax collector, Levi must have known he was hated by others. He may or may not have known about Jesus' ministry. We can only imagine what Levi must have thought when Jesus called him to join Jesus' group, but Levi did not refuse Jesus' call!

We are reminded that Jesus accepts and welcomes people no matter where they work, what they look like, or what they possess. Stand or sit where you and your child can look in the same mirror. Say, "Jesus taught us that God loves us." Sing "Jesus Loves Me" with your child. Pray, thanking God for Jesus.

Clank, clank, clank. Levi slowly dropped the coins into a box. He sat alone in the tax booth. No one wanted to talk to him because he was the tax collector.

When Jesus walked through the town, he saw Levi sitting by himself. Jesus stopped and spoke to Levi.

"Come, follow me," Jesus said.

Levi left his stack of coins and went with Jesus and his followers.

121

Jesus did not ask for volunteers when he chose the twelve disciples. And Jesus didn't choose those who we might think would be chosen—the richest, the smartest, the most popular, the best looking. Jesus chose ordinary people—people like you and me.

When Jesus chose the twelve, he saw something in each of them that other people couldn't see. Jesus saw what each person could become with God's love. The disciples didn't begin their ministry as the best preachers, teachers, or healers. But by following Jesus and learning about God, they grew in their faith.

As followers of Jesus, we too learn and grow. Talk with your child about the ways he or she has grown and the things your child has learned. Pray your thanks to God for the ways we grow and learn in the faith.

Jesus chose twelve of his followers to help him tell others about God's love.

One, two, three, four, five, six, seven, eight, nine, ten, eleven, twelve. Jesus counted the twelve special helpers. Their names were Peter, James, John, Andrew, Philip, Bartholomew, Matthew, Thomas, James, Thaddaeus, Simon, and Judas.

These followers listened to Jesus when he said, "Come! Follow me!"

Today children often wonder why the disciples were all men. Explain to your child that women did not have a prominent place in society during the time Jesus lived. As a rule, they did not attend schools or own property. In fact, they were often considered to *be* the property of their fathers or husbands.

But this didn't stop women from following Jesus. The gospel account in Luke tells us they had resources—money or possessions—that they used to help Jesus. So they, too, were important to Jesus' ministry and to Jesus' ability to travel and teach about God.

We are reminded again that Jesus called those whom others might have ignored. Jesus helped a variety of men and women see that God loved them and had a purpose for them.

Talk with your child about some of the people who are helpers in your church. Think about the janitor as well as the pastor. Say a prayer of thanks to God for all who are helpers.

Mary Magdalene's long skirt made a *swish, swish, swish* sound as she walked down the road with Joanna and Susanna. They were going to help Jesus tell others about God's love.

"Do you have the bread and the cheese, Susanna?" Joanna asked.

"Yes," said Susanna. "I have food to feed Jesus and his helpers."

Mary Magdalene smiled, "I'm glad Jesus said, 'Come! Follow me!' "

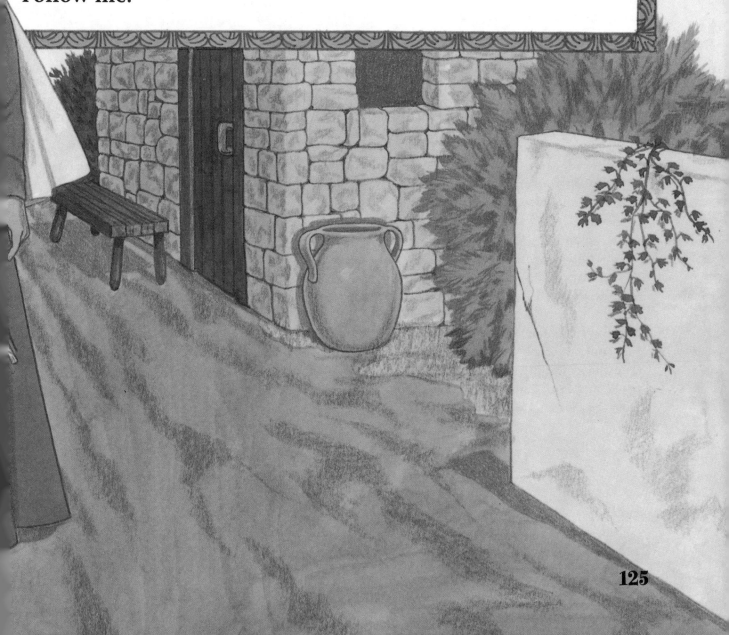

Jesus was able to reach many more people with the message of God's love by sending the disciples out two-by-two to teach others.

It is one thing to listen to a wonderful teacher, agree with the teachings, and help. It is quite another to be the person who travels from place to place teaching, preaching, and healing. When Jesus chose the twelve who would be his disciples, he asked them to do more than follow. Jesus asked them to travel the earth, preaching, teaching, and healing in his name. This must have been both exciting and frightening for the disciples, but they did as Jesus asked.

Talk with your child about a time when you were faced with a difficult task or situation and God gave you the strength to work through it. Take turns with your child, naming things the disciples needed to go and teach. You might want to name things like courage, knowledge of Jesus' teachings, trust in Jesus, and faith that God would be with them.

Shh, shh, shh. "Jesus is going to speak!"

The twelve disciples gathered quietly near Jesus.

Jesus said, "Walk to every village and town. Tell all people about God's love for them. Tell them that God wants us to treat others kindly. Help them know how to worship God."

The disciples smiled at one another. They were ready to do the work Jesus began when he asked them to, "Come! Follow me!"

Jesus said to them,
"Follow me."

Mark 1:17

Communion: A Special Meal

130

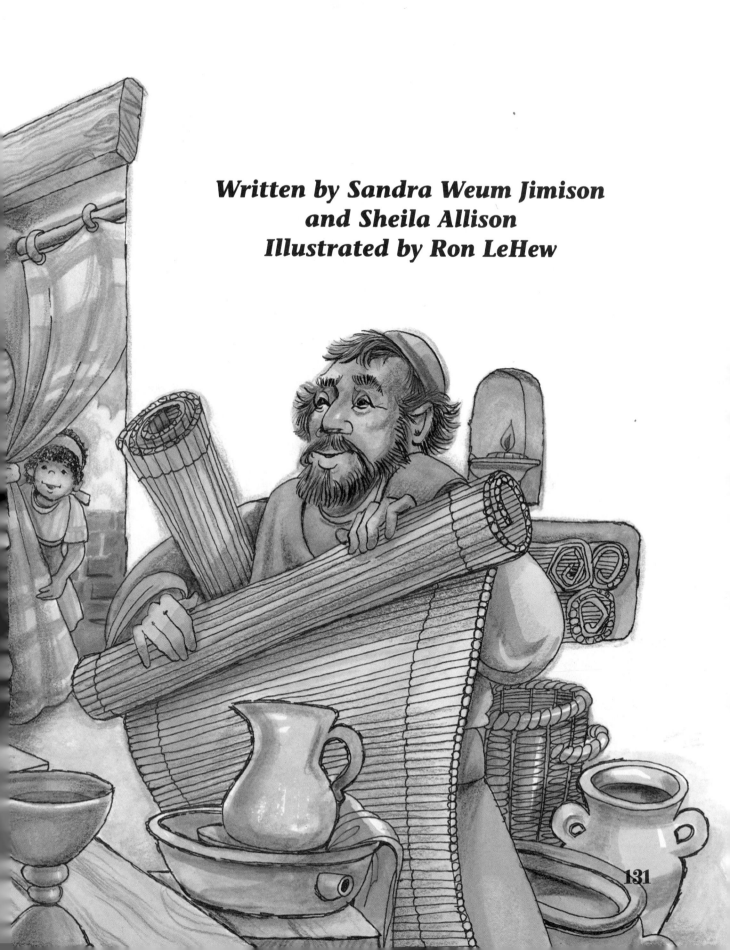

*Written by Sandra Weum Jimison
and Sheila Allison
Illustrated by Ron LeHew*

The story of Jesus' last meal with his disciples takes place during Passover. This festival will be unfamiliar to your child. Explain that Passover was a time of great celebration, much like the holidays we celebrate today. Passover is a time when Jewish people celebrate the blessing God gave them when God delivered their ancestors out of slavery in Egypt.

The history of the Passover is described in Exodus 12. When the Israelites were living in Egypt, God told Moses and Aaron that God would send a plague over the land. So that the Israelites would be protected, they put a mark of blood on the doors of their homes. The plague that God sent to Egypt "passed over" the Hebrews. Today Jewish people celebrate this and other blessings at Passover.

What a sight! People were greeting friends and family. There were donkeys, camels, and horses with carts. Merchants were selling food, pigeons, and baskets. The streets of Jerusalem were crowded with people!

133

Help your child understand the need for preparation during holidays by talking with him or her about the preparations and celebrations that your family observes for Thanksgiving. If your family usually travels to the home of a relative for the holiday, discuss the preparations needed for the trip. Then discuss the preparations needed in the home of whomever is hosting guests. Talk about ways in which your child helps with any of the preparations.

Talk with your child about the celebration of Passover. Explain that many preparations were needed for the Passover meal. The menu included roasted lamb, herbs, fruits, and nuts. Each food represented an event or a memory. Families ate the meal together. The meal was served around a low table. People sat or reclined on large cushions around the table.

families could be together to celebrate Passover."

Rachel looked around at the crowd. She had never seen so many people!

Then Benjamin whispered to Rachel, "Did you know that Jesus of Nazareth is here? He has been teaching all week. He has even been to the Temple."

"Hi, Rachel. You made it!" said Benjamin, waving to his cousin.

Rachel smiled, "Hi, Benjamin! I'm glad our

135

The meal Jesus ate with his disciples during Passover is the basis for our sacrament of Communion today. At times, the talk of "the body and blood of Christ" can be frightening. The symbolism surrounding the bread and juice confuses young children. Young children (and for that matter, most adults) cannot comprehend the mystery and beauty of the bread and the cup. It is sufficient to describe this celebration to your child as a way of our remembering a special meal Jesus ate with his friends. Communion reminds us of Jesus' love for us.

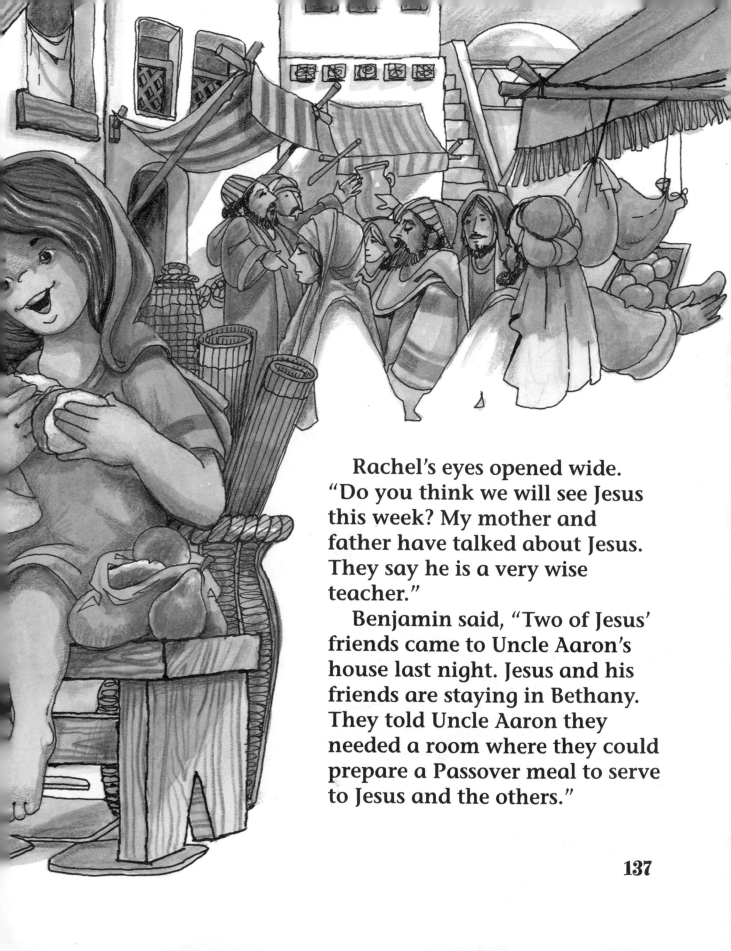

Rachel's eyes opened wide. "Do you think we will see Jesus this week? My mother and father have talked about Jesus. They say he is a very wise teacher."

Benjamin said, "Two of Jesus' friends came to Uncle Aaron's house last night. Jesus and his friends are staying in Bethany. They told Uncle Aaron they needed a room where they could prepare a Passover meal to serve to Jesus and the others."

The celebration of Communion is vital in our life together as a church body. During Communion we remember the love Jesus had for his disciples and for all people. We remember the importance of sharing what Jesus taught with others. Jesus taught the disciples the meaning of God's love and how to love others. He taught them about being faithful believers and about the importance of being together and learning from each other.

Say to your child: "Jesus taught his disciples that in all things they should give thanks to God. Jesus said that when they were eating or traveling or telling others about God, they should remember to give thanks to God. When we celebrate Communion in our church, we are remembering what Jesus taught his disciples. We are remembering that Jesus loves us and that we should love Jesus and one another."

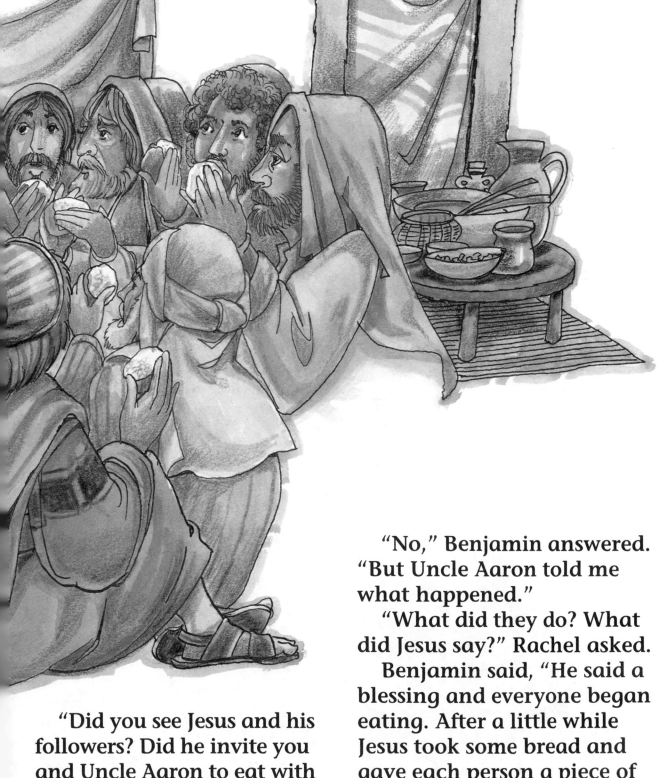

"Did you see Jesus and his followers? Did he invite you and Uncle Aaron to eat with him?" Rachel wanted to know.

"No," Benjamin answered. "But Uncle Aaron told me what happened."

"What did they do? What did Jesus say?" Rachel asked.

Benjamin said, "He said a blessing and everyone began eating. After a little while Jesus took some bread and gave each person a piece of the bread."

As adults, we readily understand that part of living includes those times when friends and family members move away, or simply lose touch, or die. When this happens, our memories of these special persons become more cherished.

Talk with your child about a friend he or she has had who has moved away. If it's appropriate, discuss the recent death of a family member or friend. Ask your child to tell you about the memories he or she has of the friend or relative. What special things did they do together? What will he or she miss about the friend or relative? Use pictures, if available, to enhance your discussion.

140

"Then what happened? Did Jesus say anything?" Rachel was curious.

Benjamin said, "Jesus took a cup from the table, and he prayed to God. Then Jesus handed the cup to everyone; they all drank from it."

"Everyone seemed sad." Benjamin said. "I think Jesus told them he would be leaving them soon. But he said that he would always love them. And he wanted them to eat the meal together to remember this night."

Communion is our celebration of Jesus' sharing a special meal with his disciples. As a sacrament, Communion reminds us of the sacrifice Jesus made for us on the cross. Communion reminds us that, as a community of faith, we are to remember Jesus and follow his example.

Talk with your child about the way in which your church celebrates Communion. If your child has received Communion, ask your child what he or she remembers about it—who blessed the bread and the juice? who served it? what was said during the celebration? If your child has not received Communion, explain how Communion is served. Tell your child what receiving Communion means for you personally.

142

Soon Uncle Aaron called Rachel and Benjamin.

"It's time for us to go to Grandfather's for our evening meal and celebration, Rachel and Benjamin," he said.

"We have been talking about Jesus," Rachel said.

"Can you tell us more about him?"

"Yes," smiled Uncle Aaron. "As we walk, I will tell you stories Jesus told of God's love."

The children held their uncle's hands as they walked and learned more about Jesus.

Jesus said,
"I give you a new commandment,
that you love one another."

John 13:34, adapted

Paul And His Friends

Written by Vicki Hines
Illustrated by Dennis Hockerman

146

Before you begin the story, talk to your child about Paul. Set the stage for the story. Explain that in the beginning of this story Paul did not like people who followed Jesus. He was angry because Jesus' friends were telling others about Jesus.

Jesus used a bright light to get Paul's attention on the road to Damascus.

Ask your child to remember a time when he or she was angry. What happened that made your child happy again?

Help your child think of some ways to diffuse anger. Suggest remembering a special Bible verse like "Love is patient; love is kind" (1 Corinthians 13:4). Talk about counting to ten before he or she says an angry word. Suggest pounding on play dough instead of hitting someone.

148

"Faster, faster," Paul urged his horse. "I'm angry. I'm going to throw all of Jesus' followers in jail."

Suddenly a bright light stopped Paul. *Kerplop*. Paul fell off his horse.

A voice said, "I am Jesus. Don't be unkind to my friends. Go to Damascus and I will tell you what to do."

Paul stood up. He could not see, but he was not angry anymore!

Help your child understand that when Jesus spoke to Paul on the road to Damascus, Paul's life was changed. Paul now wanted to *be* one of Jesus' followers.

When Paul arrived in Damascus, he still could not see and did not know what Jesus wanted him to do. He patiently waited for Jesus to show him what to do next. Are there times when your child has had to be patient? Remembering those times will help your child understand what Paul might have been feeling as he waited in Damascus.

Ananias did not know Paul, but he knew of Paul. Jesus' followers knew Paul as an unkind person who put Jesus' followers in jail. When Ananias came to heal Paul's blindness, he did not know how Paul would react. Ananias put aside his fear and did what Jesus wanted him to do.

Talk with your child about his or her fears. Are there times when your child is afraid? Encourage your child to remember Jesus' teachings when he or she is afraid.

Step, step, step. Men led Paul by the hand to Damascus. Paul waited for Jesus to tell him what to do.

Soon a stranger spoke to Paul, "I am Ananias, a follower of Jesus. Jesus has sent me to help you see again."

Ananias laid his hands on Paul's eyes. When he removed his hands, Paul could see! Paul began to tell others about Jesus.

Remind your child that being a Christian means being a follower of Jesus.

Paul and Barnabas collected money for people who did not have enough money to buy food. Does your church sponsor any mission projects that help feed the hungry? If so, make sure your child knows about your church's efforts. If your church doesn't sponsor a mission project to feed the hungry, are there opportunities in your community for your family to help feed the hungry? If your family participated in such a project, remind your child of the similarity between the project you participated in and the work that Barnabas and Paul did.

Walk, walk, walk. Paul went to Antioch where he met Barnabas. In Antioch, Jesus followers had a special name. They were called Christians.

One day Barnabas was sad. "Some of our friends have no money to buy food," he said.

"Let's ask for help," said Paul.

Clink, clink, clink. The Christians in Antioch gave coins to help.

Paul smiled, "Now all our friends can buy food." Paul and Barnabas told their friends about Jesus.

Working together is a skill that most children ages five and six have opportunities to practice. The teamwork children use in picking up toys and playing most games can easily be translated into the kind of teamwork that Paul, Aquila, and Priscilla used to make tents and to share Jesus' message.

Look for opportunities to praise your child any time you see him or her practicing teamwork skills.

154

Snip, snip, snip. Paul's scissors cut big pieces of fabric. Then he helped his friends, Priscilla and Aquila, put the pieces of fabric together to make tents.

Sew, sew, sew. The three friends worked together to make the tents. Paul, Priscilla, and Aquila also worked together to tell others about Jesus.

The river was a quiet place for Paul and his friends to pray. Does your child have a special place he or she like to pray? If not, help your child find such a place. A quiet place is best, one without a television or radio.

Quiet places are ideal for prayer, but in today's busy society, sometimes it is difficult to find a place that is completely quiet for prayer. Help your child understand that prayer happens in quiet places like church, but you can also pray in the car, in the mall, at school, and anywhere else you want to talk with God.

Splash, splash, splash. Paul and his friend Silas went to the river to pray. They sat near a woman dressed in purple.

"Do you love God?" Paul asked the woman?

"Yes," smiled the woman. "My name is Lydia. I come here to pray to God sometimes."

Paul baptized Lydia in the river that day. Lydia helped Paul and Silas tell others about Jesus.

Explain to your child that there were no telephones in Bible-times. People, like Paul, kept in touch with friends who lived far away by writing letters.

Paul's letters helped people remember Jesus' teachings. We can read Paul's letters today in the Bible to remind ourselves of Jesus' teachings.

Timothy was a young boy when he began traveling with Paul. He helped Paul write letters to other Christians.

Help your child think of ways he or she can help serve God at church and at home. Singing in the church choir and helping to put away toys at home are just two ways your child can be one of God's helpers. Can you think of more ways?

Scratch, scratch, scratch. Paul's quill pen made a scratchy sound as he and Timothy wrote a letter to Jesus' followers.

Paul and Timothy talked about their friends—Ananias, Barnabas, Priscilla, Aquila, Silas, and Lydia.

Paul prayed, "Thank you, God, for special friends. Help us tell others about Jesus."

159

A friend loves at all times.

Proverbs 17:17